For my Bisons—Jen, Ella, Cole, and Maxwell
—S.R.

For Lloyd's Barbershop
—P.O.

Random House Studio with colophon is a trademark of Penguin Random House LLC.

Visit us on the Web! rhcbooks.com

Educators and librarians, for a variety of teaching tools, visit us at RHTeachersLibrarians.com

Library of Congress Cataloging-in-Publication Data is available upon request.
ISBN 978-0-593-42817-7 (trade) — ISBN 978-0-593-42817-7 (lib. bdg.) — ISBN 978-0-593-42818-4 (ebook)

The text of this book is set in 16-point Archer Medium.
The artist used scanned gouache textures painted digitally in Photoshop to create the illustrations for this book.
Interior design by Nicole de las Heras

MANUFACTURED IN CHINA
10 9 8 7 6 5 4 3 2 1
First Edition

BLUE BISON
NEEDS A HAIRCUT

written by **Scott Rothman**   illustrated by **Pete Oswald**

RANDOM HOUSE STUDIO NEW YORK

Blue Bison liked getting haircuts because Blue Bison liked to look nice and neat for his family and playground associates.

But one day, Blue Bison couldn't get a haircut because his barber shop was closed.

Everything was closed.

The supermarket.

The ice cream shop.

The bouncy house place.

Even that weird store that sold
boogie boards for baby bison.

Why was everything closed, you ask?

Some reason.

Blue Bison didn't believe it. "Everything can't be closed," he said. "Surely everything will open back up tomorrow, and I can get a haircut then."

But Blue Bison was wrong. Everything was still closed the next day.
And the days after that. This made Blue Bison mad.

So he rammed his head into a nearby rock.

THUD!

"Hey!" Blue Bison's dad, Brown Bison, yelled. "That's my ram rock!"

Blue Bison's mom, Burgundy Bison, told them enough with
all the ramming.

"Enough with all the ramming," she said.

"But I REALLY need to get a haircut!"

"No. You WANT to get a haircut. You don't NEED to."

"I can cut your hair," said Blue Bison's little sister, Bubble Gum Bison.

But Blue Bison wasn't listening anymore. Because Blue Bison got an idea. Blue Bison went to his barber's home and offered him a deal.

"If you give me a haircut super quick, I will give you these tasty and herbaceous grasses commonly found in prairies, which we bison like to eat."

"Bison?" said the confused barber. "I thought you were a buffalo."

"I get that a lot, as we are both large, horned, ox-like creatures.
But buffalo don't have these huge humps on their shoulders or such
giant heads. They also have larger horns, though ours are much sharper."

SLAM!

But the barber wasn't listening anymore. This made Blue Bison sad.
And when bison get sad . . .

They wallow. Like so.

Blue Bison's family and playground associates tried to cheer him up.

I think you look great, honey.

Yeah, buddy, your hair is fine.

I know we are only associated with each other through our time in the playground, but we too enjoy the long length of your hair!

"I can cut your hair!" said Bubble Gum Bison,
who rolled out a lawn mower she found.

Blue Bison laughed at the idea of his little sister cutting his hair with a lawn mower because it was so utterly ridiculous. And just by laughing, Blue Bison felt a little bit better.

Blue Bison felt so good that he went out and played tag for hours with his little sister . . .

then hide and go seek . . .

then dolly smash . . .

before they both conked out for the night.

When Blue Bison woke the next day, he realized he didn't care what his hair looked like. There were more important things than having nice and neat-looking hair.

Then Blue Bison looked in the mirror.

"You like your haircut, Blue Bison?"

Mom and Dad looked at Blue Bison and waited for him to ram his head into something very hard.

"No, I don't *like* it!" Blue Bison bellowed.